Fearful Frannie

AND
HER FATEFUL TRIP TO MAUI

by
Gloria Chananie

PublishAmerica
Baltimore

First printing

ISBN: 1-4137-0162-0
PUBLISHED BY PUBLISHAMERICA, LLLP
www.publishamerica.com
Baltimore

Printed in the United States of America

Aloha!

    I must gratefully acknowledge the love and support of my family, and of my writer friends.
    Thank you Carmine, Sandy, Cecilia, Laurie, Mary Jo, Polly, Sandra and Susie.

Gloria Chananie

DOOM LOOMS

PANIC! Dad has just come home from work, and is shouting at me.

"Surprise, Frannie! I'm taking you to Hawaii, to the island of Maui. You're in for a wonderful adventure. It's a tropical paradise. Let's not forget the camera. Now run along with Helga, buy a pretty swim suit, and start packing. We're leaving in two days."

"Help, Helga," I cry, as my legs begin to shake. "I don't want to go."

Helga's our housekeeper and my best friend. The only one who really understands me. She smells sweet, like the ginger cookies she's always baking. She's getting older, but I'll love her forever. She's teaching me to cook Hungarian goulash, and how to sew.

We don't watch much TV. After school, she listens as I practice my violin, and keeps telling me I'm getting better. At night she reads her books, I read mine, and then we share. That's our special time.

Helga is plenty smart, but she keeps on insisting there's nothing to be afraid of. I know better! I've fallen off a pony, broken my arm, been bitten by a dog, stung by a yellow jacket, stuck for hours in an elevator, and once, I nearly drowned. You can see why I'm seriously afraid of animals, bugs, elevators, and water. I can't help being scared most of the time.

Dad and I live in New York City, in an apartment on the fifteenth floor. That's where I got stuck in an elevator and the firemen had to come. I don't like tall buildings or big cities.

Dad leaves home a lot, and travels all over the world. He's a diplomat and speaks four languages. He works at the UN, and is a very important person. Only trouble is, I miss him so much when he's gone. Once I got to tag along, but that's when that stupid dog bit me.

I go to Miss Merryweather's School for Girls. It's okay, but I think I'll like it better next year when I'm in the seventh grade. Dad says I'm growing up too fast. Hope I'm still alive after I grow up!

Thinking about Maui, I cry, "Dad, that island is halfway round the world. I'll get sick before I get there. You know I always get car sick."

"You don't have to worry," Dad says. "Plane rides

are smoother than cars."

"But what happens if I do get sick?" I ask, looking to Helga for support.

"You won't," Dad answers.

"How do you know?" I demand.

"You'll be fine," he says.

"How do you know?" I ask again. "When I was seven, did we know that crazy dog would bite my nose just because I wanted to pet it?"

"That was different," Dad insists. "We were in Nepal, and those dogs were specially trained to guard the temples."

"How about last year when that fat dude decided to do a cannonball into the pool and landed on me? I nearly drowned before they saw me. Remember?" I say.

Helga, stifling a snicker, interrupts, "My little schnitzel, Hawaii is a beautiful place. You'll love it, yah?" Stretching out her plump arm, she pulls me to her side. Her wiry gray hair tickles my cheek.

"Will you come too?" I beg. Helga really is my best friend. "What if I get stuck in another elevator? I spent four hours in that smelly box. The only reason the firemen came was because you couldn't find me and called 911. I might have spent my whole life in there, if it hadn't been for you."

Helga smiles warmly as she asks, "Who will feed

your goldfish? There is much to keep me busy here. Just don't you forget to write me postcards."

THE ARRIVAL

Miracles do happen, I guess. I don't get sick, and the plane lands okay. A bunch of happy natives with flowered shirts meet us at the airport. They almost smother me to death piling orchid leis around my neck as they sing, "Aloha, Aloha!"

The sun's shining…why am I so nervous?

A fancy limousine drives us to our hotel. This I can take. They lead us to our suite, where Dad quickly points out, "See, Frannie? It's on the first floor. No need for elevators."

What a relief! *He really does love me*, I think. Loaded with flowers, our rooms smell like a perfume factory. I spot a bowl of fruit on my night stand, and a neat fridge next to my dresser.

"Dad, look," I call, checking out the fridge. "Yum — my favorite chocolate bars. Hey, found some peanuts, drinks — lots of goodies!"

What a view from our window. Only the blue-green Pacific Ocean as far as the eye can see. We can open our patio doors and walk onto the beach if we want to. I don't! I'm hungry and tired, so I peel a banana, pull the drapes closed, and flop into bed.

Next morning, Dad grabs his briefcase and runs off to meetings. Flying out the door, he calls, "Frannie, I'm sorry, but you'll have to amuse yourself for a little while. Visit the lobby. It's a beauty. I'll meet you there later with a nice surprise."

He's gone.

That's my dad.

Hmmm — wondering what his surprise will be, I decide to check out the lobby. But first, I write a postcard to Helga and tell her I'm still alive.

The lobby's filled with fancy shops. Not for kids. Tons of tropical plants are everywhere. Interesting, but not for kids. Huge cages filled with birds stretch toward the ceiling. It looks like they've been splashed with crazy, mixed-up colors. They're singing their hearts out. Oooo — this I love!

The sign on the cage says, 'Parrots, Macaws, and Hawaiian Nenes.' Hard for me to tell which is which.

"Hi, birdies," I tweet.

I sit down by a palm tree, listen to the birds, and wait for Dad.

I hear yacking on the other side of my palm tree. People in matching T-shirts are all excited about something. I can only make out, *Maui, humpback whales and dolphins.*

As I get up to look for my dad, I feel a hand on my shoulder. I spin around to look up into a pretty, tanned face with sparkling eyes.

"Aloha! Welcome to Maui, Frannie. I'm Wanda, the scuba instructor. Your dad said I would find you here. Ready for some scuba lessons? You look like you'd be interested in learning something new."

You've got to be kidding, I think. I'm polite as I say, "No, thank you, I don't think so."

Happy to hear Dad calling me, I quickly rush over to him. Shocked, I listen as he calls to her and says, "Aloha, Wanda, meet my daughter Frannie."

Digging the toe of my sandal deep into the carpet, I lower my eyes. "We've met," I mumble.

Talking fast, Dad says, "Frannie, I've arranged for you to have scuba lessons with Wanda. Her parents own a dive shop near Hana, on the other side of the island. They taught your mother and I how to dive when we came to Maui on our honeymoon. I've known Wanda since she was a baby. All grown up, she's now a certified dive instructor. She'll look after you while I'm working. You'll be perfectly safe with her. Have fun, and I'll see you at dinner."

Dad seems so pleased with his surprise, I don't have the heart to say, no way! At least not yet.

Looking at Wanda's friendly, face, I decide I will meet her after lunch. I don't want to be alone again. I think, *well, maybe I could use a new friend.*

Wanda says, "I'm glad your dad signed you up, Frannie. I know we'll be friends...like sisters. Let's go to the pool this afternoon. I'll introduce you to your scuba gear and teach you the basics. You'll be a pro in no time. Pick you up after lunch."

"Sounds like she can use a friend too," I tell myself.

THE TERROR BEGINS

Did I say, I'd meet her? What was I thinking? No way can I go through with it. I've heard stories. People can die scuba diving.

I decide to have lunch. This will give me time to think, and come up with a good excuse not to go. I tell the waitress, "I'm not too hungry. Just give me a double cheeseburger with onion and tomato, large fries, a strawberry milkshake, and one of those macadamia nut brownies."

In the dining room, I see those dudes in the matching T-shirts from the lobby. They're having lunch and whispering. 'Save the Whales' is splashed across their shirts. The fat lady in the baseball cap waves like she knows me. Being polite, I sorta smile back.

I finish eating, sign the check, and head to my room,

never looking back. I need to think fast. Maybe I'll have an attack of stomach flu, or a terrible headache. I could fall and sprain my ankle, or break something — anything!

As I dream up excuses, I don't pay attention to where I'm going. Turning a corner, I whack my head. I see stars! Am I bleeding? Maybe I cracked my skull. No such luck! I've only given myself a bad mood.

I don't really need the big Band-Aid I glue above my eye, but it looks impressive. Maybe when Wanda sees it, she'll let me off easy.

I flop on my bed, and think of more excuses. Hearing a knock at the door, I break into a cold sweat. I really do feel sick!

"Who is it?" I call, knowing full well who it is.

"It's me, Wanda," she answers cheerfully. Too cheerful for me! "Time to go to the pool. No excuses! I'm here to prove there's nothing to fear. Trust me," she says.

I wonder what she knows about me. Has Dad told her of all I've been through?

I hear myself saying, "Wait a minute."

I forget all about excuses as I slip into my new swim suit. I even sling a beach robe over my shoulders. I never intended to use either of them, but here I am, letting myself be led into a pool. My worst nightmare!

Wanda can't help but notice my big Band-Aid, and

asks, "Poor Frannie, how on earth did you get that? Does it hurt?"

"Hit a wall, and yes it hurts," I answer, glad that she's noticed. I think, *a perfect excuse if I change my mind.* "I'm hoping the pain won't last too long."

The pool is empty except for two little kids and their mom. Laughing and splashing, they toss a big red ball to each other at the shallow end.

I can throw a ball! I call, "Hello," but they ignore me. How I wish I could join them.

Wanda lines up all the gear by the edge at the deep end, and starts to explain what I must do.

As I try to pull on the wetsuit, I say, "Wanda, I'm feeling faint."

She smiles.

She helps me on with the flippers, and I tell her, "I'm going to barf."

She laughs.

She belts weights around my waist, and I say, "They're too heavy. I'm going to fall on my face."

She laughs again.

By the time she straps the air tank onto my back and tries to shove a mouthpiece between my lips, my mouth locks like a steel trap. She gets the message as I scream, "I can't swim, I don't want to die!"

Softly, she says, "Frannie, sit down next to me and relax. Your dad told me you've had three years of swimming lessons. Let me assure you that I will not let you die. I promise to keep you safe every moment. I will not leave your side. When you're ready, I want you to put on your face mask. Let me show you how easy it is."

In full gear, she eases over the edge into the pool, and beckons for me to follow.

My heart is pounding hard. Funny thing though, I feel a little excited. I also feel foolish in all the stupid gear. I look like an alien. That thought makes me giggle.

I put on the face mask, and call, "I'm coming." Slipping on the wet tiles...I flop head first into the water. How humiliating!

When I come splashing to the top, I see that group of 'Save the Whales' people watching me. They probably wanna save me too.

Wanda holds my arms. Even with all the weight, I'm not drowning. She hands me the mouth piece and says, "Frannie, breathe through this."

She turns a valve on the tank, and I taste sweet, fresh air rush into my mouth. I feel dizzy and cling to her for dear life. When I open my eyes underwater, I see Wanda, and feel better.

I'm not doing too well. I keep sinking to the bottom of the pool. I start to flip my flippers real fast, and that helps. I wonder if a fish ever has this problem.

Wanda keeps her word and never leaves my side. It's almost dinner time before we surface for the last time and she says, "Enough for one day. I can't believe what a natural you are, Frannie. You'll be ready for the ocean in a few days."

I can't wait to write Helga about the cool things I've done today. She'll be so excited.

Wait a minute, did she say ocean? And WE?

It's dinner time, and I've thrown away my Band-Aid. Dad shouldn't know what a big klutz I've been.

"I had a really fun time today," I tell Dad. "I didn't drown!"

Dad smiles and says, "Frannie, you have no idea how pleased I am. My business is taking longer than I expected. Now I won't have to worry about you having a good time. Enjoy your lessons with Wanda, and later in the week I'll show you around Maui."

That evening Dad and I walk barefoot on the beach. The sand sparkles in the moonlight. Our toes scrunch deep into the warm, wet sand. As I lick the salty spray from my lips, I hear something.

I say, "Listen, Dad. What is that?"

"It's only the pounding surf," he answers.

On the moonlit ocean, I think I see dolphins playing near the shore. I'm sure I see whales too. Do I hear singing? Is it the dolphins and whales, or the pounding surf that keeps repeating over and over, "You're learning a lot, *Crash n' Splash*, so laugh a lot, *Crash n' Splash,* Wanda's near, *Crash n' Splash*, nothing to fear, *Crash n' Splash.*"

FEAR? WHAT'S THAT?

Next morning, I crunch an apple and a chocolate bar from the fridge. I slip into my swim suit, grab my robe, and head for the pool. I can't believe it. I want to be with my new friend and try scuba diving again.

I look everywhere. Wanda isn't here! I'd been so ready. Now I am starting to feel scared again, and I start to cry.

Those whale people are sitting across the pool. Are they watching me? They bother me. Everything bothers me. I may have been afraid before, but now I'm hurt and mad.

Marching over to them, I blurt out, "Don't you have something better to do than stare at me? You don't even know me!"

Standing up, the lady in the baseball cap says, "Honey, we're sorry if we upset you. We just thought

you looked a little lonely and might like to join us on
our whale watch."

I feel pretty stupid and sputter, "I'm really sorry I
yelled at you. I'm waiting for my friend. She's late.
She's teaching me to scuba dive."

Spinning around to leave, I run smack into Wanda.
Her arms are loaded with our gear. Everything flies
into the air and the pool.

Embarrassed, I say, "I'm sorry. I'll help pick up."

Wanda laughs as she rescues flippers and face
masks from the pool. "Did you think I wasn't
coming?" she says, piling our stuff on the edge of the
pool. "You weren't leaving, were you?"

I notice the whale people are gone, and say, "Wanda,
those weirdos bother me. They want me to join them
watch whales."

We put on our wetsuits. "They aren't weirdos,"
Wanda says. "Just ordinary people who want to save
the whales and dolphins."

Tightening my belt for me, she explains, "They
come here every year for the humpback whales'
migrating season. They sit on the beach and watch,
always with their cameras and binoculars. Don't let
them bother you. They mean well."

"Okay," I say. "I guess I'm just being a dork."

Soon I forget about them and concentrate on my
lesson. I keep doing it all wrong. I'm ready to quit a

thousand times. "Phooey," I moan. "I'll never learn! It's too hard."

Wanda won't let me stop. "Try it again, Frannie," she keeps urging. "You're getting it."

Little by little, I get the hang of it. I'm so excited. "Wow, Wanda, this is really great. Thank you!"

"Don't thank me," she says. "You're the one who's doing it."

Was I really doing it?

Yes, I am! I can sink to the bottom, rise to the top, and once I even did a handstand. I'm as light as a beach ball.

With Wanda by my side, I feel safe. I don't want the lesson to end. But it does when Wanda says, "It's almost dinner time."

How fast the day has gone! My swim suit has hardly gotten wet. Best of all, I'm not scared in the water anymore. I can't wait to tell Dad, and write Helga.

As we get ready to leave, Wanda says, "Frannie, you're amazing. After only two days, I think you're almost ready. Since we've really become like sisters, I want to share a secret with you."

It feels good to be called her sister. "Super," I reply. "Secret is my middle name. Tell me, what is it?"

"I've found a wreck on the ocean floor," Wanda confides. "But we'll have to check your diving skills before we go down together."

"A wreck? Jewels? Treasures?" I can't wait to tell Helga. Oh no! I can't. It's a secret.

"Her name is *Lucky Lady*," Wanda tells me. "I've got a sturdy motorboat that we can dive from. You can't imagine how beautiful the sunrise is on the water. You'll never forget it. I'd love to take you with me. If your father agrees, will you come?"

Suddenly, I get a splitting headache. "Wanda," I moan. "You're talking about the ocean. The big Pacific Ocean! It's filled with strange creatures and man-eating sharks. I'll bet the crabs can bite through our wetsuits."

She replies, "You're going to love it. We'll have such fun together. I promise."

As I start to say no, the chant from the roaring surf rings in my ears. "*Learning a Lot, Laughing a Lot, Wanda is Near, Nothing to Fear.*"

Slowly, my fear drains away. Like someone has pulled the plug. It was a good feeling. I hear myself laugh as I say, "Okay, Wanda!"

THE LULL BEFORE THE STORM

The next few days are the greatest! I practice with Wanda in the mornings, and Dad takes me sightseeing in the afternoons. He buys me a Hawaiian dress called a sarong, with four strands of white, jingling shells that dangle around my neck.

The sales lady tucks a delicate red flower into my hair, and says, "This is a hibiscus blossom, our Hawaiian state flower. Now, don't you feel like a native?"

Yes, I do...and I like it.

Dad says, "Let's play tourist," and takes me into an old whaling town called Lahina. It has the biggest Banyon tree in the world. I mean, it is huge!

In the harbor, we climb onboard an ancient whaling ship. How could those sailors have stood it? Below deck it's dark and gross. Small and smelly. It's like being in that elevator again. My head hits the ceiling. "Ouch!"

Dad says the sailors would spend many months on that little boat. Bummer! I can't wait to get out of here.

On the wharf, I notice a grungy old man. He reminds me of a pirate. His white hair and beard are long and stringy. He even has a peg leg. Sitting on the far end of the pier, he's just staring out to sea.

"Look, Dad," I say as I giggle. "He's got a peg leg. Do you think an alligator ate his real one? Like Captain Hook?"

Sternly, Dad says, "Now, Frannie, don't be mean and quick to judge."

I feel guilty, and say, "Sorry." But that old man really does look like a pirate.

We leave the pier and wander down the street to the straw market.

"Look, Dad," I say. "I love this straw hat. It fits perfectly. Can I have it?"

He likes it too, and says, "Yes, indeed." He bought the hat for me, and a big one for Helga. She'll look super in it.

Several shops are selling scrimshaw. I love what the old whalers have made. They've carved all kinds of shapes from whale bone and ivory. Then they etched and painted beautiful, colorful designs all over them.

I can't resist asking, "Dad, can we buy this comb for Helga? She'll flip!"

"Sure," he replies. "It'll look great in Helga's hair."

For lunch, Dad makes me taste a fish called mahi-mahi. I don't like fish, but it's delicious! I eat every bite. I love the fried bananas, mangoes, and the yummy fruit drinks at the open-air restaurants. The drinks are served in coconut shells with tiny umbrellas stuck in the middle.

I ask Dad, "Don't you wish you could buy these drinks in New York City?"

He laughs and says, "Yes, maybe one day we will."

Being good tourists, we take a ride on an antique train. It chugs all the way to a huge pineapple plantation, where row after row of pineapples stretch as far as we can see. The workers give us chunks of fresh pineapple to eat for free. Juicy and sweet as sugar.

Going back to town, a tropical shower blows in. "Hold your horses," I shout. "Wait 'till I pull my hat down over my face," but I get soaked anyway.

When the storm ends, the most beautiful rainbow fills the sky. "Dad," I say, as I brush off the remaining rain drops, "this must really be paradise. I'll bet there's a pot of gold here someplace. I'm sorry Helga isn't here to see it."

"Don't worry, Frannie, I'm taking lots of pictures

to show her when we get home."

It's the fourth afternoon, and Dad really scares me. He says, "Frannie, today we'll see Maui from the air. We're going to take a trip in a helicopter."

When I say I'm scared, I mean I'm *really* scared. I had almost forgotten about my dumb fears. This will be ten times worse than being stuck in a stinky elevator.

I start to shake, and beg, "Dad, *please* don't make me do this!"

He only smiles, pats my head, and tells me, "Frannie, you'll love it. You may never have this opportunity again. I insist."

When Dad insists, he always gets his way. I have no choice. "Remember, Dad, it was you who sent me to my doom," I groan.

At the heliport, I stare at the big bug with no wings. As the pilot gives me a boost into my seat, I snarl, "Who in their right mind would fly in this thing?"

The answer comes from Dad, scrunched in the back seat. "You and me, that's who."

The propellers twirl, and up we go! Forever, we seem to sit still in the sky. I check with my stomach. It's doin' okay. This is easier than I expected.

Slowly, we float over trees and rooftops. The pilot is busy describing the sights. He really knows his island. I hadn't paid much attention to the big mountain in the background before. I had been concentrating on water. This is pretty cool, too.

Suddenly, we lift straight up, higher and higher, to the top of the mountain. "I can't believe it, I'm not sick!" I say. "First I was a fish, now I'm a bird."

The pilot tells us, "The volcano below is called Haleapala. It hasn't erupted for thousands of years. It's 10,000 feet high and twenty miles wide. The crater is 3,000 feet deep and filled with lava rock, vegetation, and wild life. Incidentally, Maui is called the Valley Island."

"That's one big mountain," Dad says.

"With a really big valley," I add.

On the other side of the island, we float above the most magnificent waterfalls. From up in the sky, they look like silver ribbons rippling down jagged cliffs into the blue-green sea.

Dad points to the island of Molokai in the distance. "Long ago," he tells me, "Molokai was used as a leper colony. Known as the forbidden island, no healthy person was allowed to visit. Leprosy was contagious, and, in those days, there was no cure." Dad knew some other facts too, but they only made me sad for the poor, lonely lepers.

This night, I write a long letter to Helga. A postcard will not hold it all.

SINK OR SWIM

"Dad, was that a knock at the door?" I ask.

"It's Wanda," Dad announces.

I wonder what she and Dad are talking about? I can't wait to tell Wanda about the helicopter, and how I flew like a bird.

"Frannie," Dad calls, "Wanda had to leave, but she wanted me to tell you that tomorrow is your big day. Be ready by five in the morning. She'll pick you up here. I think this is a great opportunity. I wish I could be in your shoes."

I don't think he really means it, 'cause he told me to be quiet and not wake him in the morning.

My alarm rings. It's four-thirty. Half-asleep, I munch on a ripe pear and a chocolate bar. I love-love-love chocolate!

I'm ready by five and dressed in my suit, when the

knock comes at my door. My heart is racing. I feel dizzy and sorta fluttery. Wanda's smiling face soon puts an end to that, and off we go.

Wanda seems in a hurry. I'm not, but I stumble along to keep up. We follow a trail that leads through a tangled grove of palm trees. The winding path opens onto a sun-lit beach. In front of us lies the most peaceful lagoon — no pounding surf, just a gentle lapping on the polished white sand.

The view knocks me out. It's a picture postcard! The sky's an icy blue.

A slow, rising sun is warming it up, with rays of pink, purple, gold and orange. A blanket of cotton clouds hangs over us, like a fluffy comforter.

"Oooooooh, Wanda," I say, "we're smack in the middle of a painting, and it's a masterpiece!"

"I knew you would love it," she replies.

Moored to a creaky, old, weather-beaten dock, Wanda's boat seems sturdy enough as it bobs, straining on its line.

We put on our wetsuits. "Here I go," I say swallowing hard. "I'm stepping into this boat and into the unknown."

Wanda laughs.

Without another word, we speed into deep waters. The only sound comes from the purring motor as it slices through the mirror-like surface. Searching the horizon, I find nothing to look at, not even the smallest boat. Behind us the shore disappears. The water gets choppier as we plow further out into the ocean.

Finally, Wanda turns off the motor, drops anchor and begins to strap on the rest of her gear.

"Frannie, let me help you with yours," she says. "We have one hour's supply of air, so there's plenty of time to explore the wreck below. Remember two things. One, we're diving buddies, so stay close to me, and two, don't touch anything unless I say that it's okay. Ready? Let's go!"

I wonder, *am I ready? What about my fears? Wanda expects so much from me. Can I swim well enough? Am I the same Frannie that came to Maui only a few days ago?"*

In that split second before the fearful Frannie hits the water, my doubts return. I think, *IDIOT, what are you doing?*

As I dive beneath the surface with Wanda by my side, a new *Fearless Frannie* laughs and thinks, *Here I come water world!*

Wowee! Nothing could have prepared me for what I see. Unbelievable! Beautiful! Spectacular! The ocean's bottom is pretty far down, but I can see it clearly beneath the crystal water. There are coral reefs of every color and shape. Like hula dancers, sea plants are waving at me. Flashing and flitting, there are schools of curious fish showing off their wildly decorated bodies. They blow my mind. This world of water teems with magic — beyond my imagination. I love being here.

My eyes lock onto a bouquet of pretty pink flowers, transparent as cellophane. They remind me of the pink tissue roses I once made for Helga when I was in Brownies. As we swim by, as a keepsake for Helga, I simply can't resist picking one.

Too late, I remember Wanda's warning. Do not touch anything! A blast of hot pain shoots through my right hand. I've been stung by that beautiful flower!

NEAR DEATH EXPERIENCE?

My throbbing hand has turned to bright red and a dull purple. I cry out painfully, "Wanda, Wanda, help me!"

She can't hear me, but she sees I'm in trouble. Grabbing hold of me, she pushes me to the surface.

"Look at my hand!" I moan as we return to shore. "It's a purple eggplant with fat fingers. I'll never go back," I sob. "I should have known something like this would happen."

Wanda remains calm as she leads me back to the hotel. She explains that I have been stung by a poisonous pink sea anemone! It wasn't a beautiful flower at all, but a deadly sea creature.

A doctor comes to the rescue.

Terrified, I ask him, "Doctor, am I going to die?"

He puts gunk on my wounds, packs my hand in

ice, and tells me, "Take two aspirin, and I'll see you in the morning."

I wonder, *is he a real doctor? Is he color blind? Does he see the same purple that I do?*

Dad is soon at my side. After speaking with the doctor, he says, "Frannie, the doctor says you are young and strong. In a couple of days, you'll be back in the water. You had a scare, but it was an accident. Don't let this spoil your trip."

Dad is not sympathetic, and I tell him so. "You don't understand. I can never go back in the water! I just can't."

Later, I fall asleep, with fishy nightmares swimming in my head.

I awaken the next day, shaking all over. Dad expects me to go back. I won't do it! My hand doesn't really hurt too much. It's not purple anymore, but it's still red and a little swollen.

The doctor shows up early, and says, "You're almost as good as new."

I'm going to sue him, I tell myself. *He's a quack!*

Dad has waited to hear what the doctor has to say, and seems relieved. Before leaving for his conference, he says, "Frannie, my dear, take it easy today. Keep ice on your hand and I'll meet you for lunch."

I mutter in my weakest voice, "Okay, Dad, if I feel stronger."

"I know you will," he says. "See you later."

Later that morning, I am feeling better. Bored, I decide to hang out in the lobby. I prop up my right elbow with my left hand. That not only protects my injury, but also, people can see how bad it is.

I forget about my hand when I see Wanda running into the lobby. A little out of breath, she says, "Frannie, you're looking good. Glad you're up and about. Boy, have I had a busy morning. I just returned from the Maritime offices. I checked the registry for *Lucky Lady*. Found out she was lost in the '40s…after Pearl Harbor. Maybe a connection, maybe not."

"What's Pearl Harbor?" I ask.

"December 7, 1941, was the start of World War II. Pearl Harbor was our naval port in Hawaii. After it was bombed by the Japanese in a surprise attack, America entered World War II," she answers.

"I guess that was before I was born," I say.

"Yes, fortunately it was, and for me too," she replies.

Wanda pauses, then adds, "There's some mystery about the owner of *Lucky Lady*. Except for the United States government in 1946, no claim or inquiry was ever made. The ship was registered under the name 'Lucky'. The good news is, I've been given a license to dive for the salvage. Even more exciting, I ran into the old harbor master, Jake. He was working in Maui in the '40s. He's agreed to meet me here this afternoon at two o'clock. Says he has a lot to tell me. Who knows? He may be able to shed some light on our mystery ship. I expect you to come too."

A meeting? I think, a*s long as it was going to be held above water.*

"That'll be okay," I say.

THE MEETING

I never get a chance to say much more. Dad shows up and asks, "How are you feeling, Frannie?"

Weakly I answer, "Maybe a little better."

When Dad sees Wanda, he put his arm around her shoulders, like a long-lost friend, and says, "Wanda, join us for lunch and fill me in on your family."

Turning to me he says, "Frannie, your mom and I returned often to Maui and shared many good times with Wanda's parents. I remember when Wanda was born. My, how time flies."

The two of them yack and yack about Wanda's family, the *Lucky Lady* and all kinds of other stuff.

I feel ignored.

Dad finally turns to me and says, "Frannie, this is the sort of thing you can write a report on when you return to school. I know you'll feel up to going down to the wreck tomorrow. I'll be anxious to hear all about it."

"We'll see, Dad," I say reluctantly. "We'll see."

Dad leaves for his meeting, and Wanda leads me outside to wait for Jake on the terrace. I'm not feeling left out anymore.

"What exactly do you think he can tell us?" I ask Wanda.

"Hard to say, but I'm anxious to find out. He seemed eager to talk when I spoke to him this morning."

My heart jumps into my throat when I see Jake walking toward us. I should say, hobbling. It's the old man Dad and I saw on the pier in Lahina!

I whisper to Wanda, "He looks scary, like a real pirate."

Wanda says, "Hush!" as she turns to greet him. She shakes his hand and says, "Glad you could make it, Jake. Let me introduce you to my friend, Frannie."

The grizzled old harbormaster still reminds me of Captain Hook. He smells like the sea. Quickly, he sets my mind at ease with his hearty belly laugh. I like it when he reaches for my hand and shakes it, like I'm a grownup. His firm grip hurt a little. I think he looks like a jolly, white-haired, one-legged cartoon character. I want to ask him how he lost his leg, but think better of it.

In a deep, raspy voice, he bellows, "Ahoy thar,

mates," and flops onto his chair.

"Jake," Wanda asks, "what can you tell us about the *Lucky Lady*?"

"T'was a long time ago," he says. "But I tell ye I remember it well."

We listen closely. "*Lucky Lady* was a two-masted schooner, rigged fore and aft. A sea-worthy pleasure craft, she was."

"Who owned the ship?" Wanda asks.

Stomping his peg leg on the floor and slapping his knees, he says, "Knew 'em well. Real friendly people. T'was DJ Harwell and his pretty wife, Lucy. He always called her 'Lucky'. Matter of fact, Lucy looked a lot like you, Miss Frannie. They retired to these islands, just a'fore the Japanese bombed Pearl Harbor."

"Did they have any children?" Wanda asks anxiously.

"Nary a one," he answers. "That's probably why they volunteered to be spotters for the U.S. Navy. Ole DJ rigged his boat with a new-fangled wireless radio, and off they sailed. Cruised the islands checkin' on the movement of enemy ships, they did. Heard they helped the Navy to search 'n destroy a whole bunch of Japanese war ships. Good spies. Deservin' of a medal, if you ask me. Don't think they ever got one, though."

Wanda appears relieved as she asks, "So they were

real heroes?"

"Reckon they were," Jake says. "Risked their lives every day. Never knew what happened to 'em, or the *Lucky Lady*, till this very day."

"What sank her?" I finally pipe up.

"Don't know, Miss Frannie. Could've been an enemy sub, but most likely a typhoon. Seen plenty of 'em in my day. These waters are full of ships blown onto the reefs, hit by a typhoon, or maybe even a tidal wave."

Wanda says, "Jake, we can't thank you enough for all your help. It's not often one gets the history of a ship along with its salvage rights."

Jake laughs and says, "Good luck with your salvage, Miss. Don't reckon you'll find much of value, though. The *Lucky Lady* traveled light so's to outfox and outrun the enemy." He scratches his beard and adds, "Never met a woman a'fore who salvaged anythin'. You're a right brave 'un, you are."

Wanda smiles at me as she tells him, "Frannie and I are going to have a wonderful adventure. Who knows, we might get lucky."

Remembering the pink sea anemone, I say, "I sure hope so."

NOW WHAT?

Another perfect, sunny day in Maui, but I don't want to get out of bed.

A knock at the door calls me to action. My leg has fallen asleep. Limping, I open the door for Wanda.

"How does the deep sea diver feel today?" Wanda asks. "Did something happen to your leg?"

"It's asleep," I mumble.

"How's the rest of you?" she asks with a smile.

"I'm not sure," I answer.

"Are you ready for our adventure? Your hand looks better."

"Come back later, Wanda. I'll let you know then," I say. "I'm still not sure if I ever want to go back in the water."

"Okay," Wanda smiles. "I'll come back when *Fearless* Frannie wakes up."

My demons are yelling, "*Something terrible is going to happen. You know you always attract trouble. Look what happened the day before yesterday. Don't go!*"

I hear Helga's voice. "*Sweet schnitzel, this is a chance to prove you can do it. I have faith in you. You must try!*"

My hand doesn't hurt anymore, and the swelling is gone. What's my excuse? A battle heats up in my head. Seems I've been going to war my whole life.

I'm getting fed up!   I hear a new voice yelling, "Frannie, you twit! Get a life!" That voice is mine! The voice of a *Fearless* Frannie!

When Wanda returns with our wet suits I say, "Okay, Wanda. You win! I'm tired of putting on this stupid suit, but I'm ready to try again. It *was* beautiful down there, *wasn't* it?"

Wanda takes my hand and says, "You betcha! Let's go."

THE DISCOVERY!

I'm gliding to the floor of the ocean. Only this time, I hold my hands close to my body. I relax and enjoy the friendly fish. Once again, they are in all their glory, trailing streaks of neon light. I remember to watch Wanda. I see her signaling for me to follow. I can make out the skeleton of a sunken ship. Its bones are covered with sand and sea glop, only a few yards away. Awesome!

Fish scatter around us as we swim together to inspect the barnacle-covered wreck. Looking sideways, I can make out the letters on the tilted bow. *LUCKY LADY.*

Wanda signals for me to halt. She reaches into what must have been the cabin, and lifts the rusty remains of an old radio. Putting it back, she moves on to another spot — I think the galley. Carefully, she digs through piles of debris. She lifts a large piece of the hull. Yuck! It's all rotted and crawling with sea worms.

Underneath, something is half buried in the sand. It looks like a wooden box. Wanda nods for me to pick it up. I try, but it's too heavy. Wanda moves the large piece of rotted wood to one side and slowly pulls the box from the sand. With thumbs up, she motions for us to return to the surface.

I'm so excited! Have we found a real treasure?

After we flop back into the boat, "You're safe now box," I say, as I take off my face mask. "We've rescued you from a watery grave."

Wanda sets the box on the floor of the boat. She pulls out a little pick and begins chipping off the barnacles.

I hold my breath. She pries the lid off. "Is it a treasure, Wanda? Is it?" I ask.

Without a word, she slowly lifts up several waterlogged pictures, and carefully spreads them out on the floor of the boat.

When she speaks, there are tears in her eyes. "These are pictures of Lucy and DJ as they looked long ago. It's so sad. This is all that remains of their life. Just a big, wet pile of papers and a few old dollar bills and coins."

Some treasure, I think.

"Wait a minute," Wanda says. "There's something

else at the very bottom."

She pulls out a long, golden chain with a small gold locket dangling at the end.

"It IS a treasure!" I squeal. Breathlessly, I beg, "Open the locket, Wanda. Open it up!"

After prying it open, Wanda hands it to me so I can see, too. I slowly read, and then read it again. The inscription inside says, *'Lucky You'*. I hold the locket in my hand. With all my heart I want it to be mine. But I know better.

A TIME TO THINK!

"Wanda," I say, "my whole world has flipped upside down since I met you. Now, I'm more curious than afraid. So many exciting things have happened. Tell me, why does the *Lucky Lady* seem so special?"

Wanda answers, "Of all the wrecks in this ocean, I think we were led to the *Lucky Lady* for a reason. Don't you feel like DJ and Lucy wanted us to find them? They were lost and forgotten. Besides Jake, no one else remembers. After all these years, we are the ones who can finally say, *Thank you for all you did for our country.*"

Walking back to the hotel I say, "We can't give them a medal, but we can give them flowers."

"Frannie, that's a super idea. Let's go out one more time," Wanda suggests. "Your dad says tomorrow is your last day in Maui. So it will be our last chance to visit *Lucky Lady* and say goodbye to her."

"I'll meet you at dawn," I say. I like playing this detective stuff, but I don't think I'll mention this to Dad. At least not yet.

THE LUAU

For our last night on Maui, Dad takes me to a Hawaiian luau. What a party! The beach is all lit up with flaming torches. In honor of the occasion, I wear my sarong and clinking shell beads.

"Look, Dad," I say. "Look at those hula dancers in grass skirts. Don't you love the way they swish and sway? That's how the coral waves to me from the ocean floor. How about those dudes dancing with fire sticks? Listen to the beat of those island drums and ukuleles. This music is to die for!"

"I'm glad you're enjoying it, Frannie," Dad says. "It is a paradise, isn't it?"

Inhaling mouth-watering smells, I agree and ask. "Have you ever seen so much food — Is that a pig in the fire pit with an apple in its mouth?"

"Yes. Hawaiian luaus are famous for their delicious

roasted pig,"

"Yuck! Poor pig." I lose my appetite. "I think I'm going to barf," I gag.

Dad smiles, saying, "Have some poi. You'll like it."

"Give me a break, Dad!" I say.

Dad says, "Try it — c'mon!"

"Oh, all right. Just a taste," I agree.

With a delicious mouthful, I tell him, "Dad, you can't imagine how beautiful it is under water. I'm really looking forward to going out with Wanda one last time."

Dad says, "I'm glad you and Wanda have become such close friends. Now, let me tell you about my meetings. The delegates are close to an agreement. Things have gone well. Tomorrow, we should wrap it all up."

"Super," I say, as I nibble on a hot, sweet potato dripping with butter. He is feeling good about his negotiations. I let him talk, grateful not to have to say anything more. All I can think about is tomorrow.

LET COME WHAT MAY!

Five o'clock on the button. The familiar rap comes to my door. I'm ready. This time I have plenty of flowers in my hand. I've picked the prettiest ones from the bouquets in our room.

We walk the long path to the lagoon. Wanda's boat is waiting for us at the dock.

"Look at that sunrise, Wanda," I exclaim. "Is it for real? Look at those fingers of squiggly colors. They look like crayons coloring the sky." I am even thinking like a poet. Helga isn't going to believe it.

Wanda smiles, "This scene is a gift you'll remember long after you return home."

Yes, I'll remember this...and a whole lot more, I think.

After pulling on our wet suits, we head out toward the deep water to say our last good-byes to DJ, Lucy, and the *Lucky Lady*.

As I glance back at the shore, I see the whale people setting up a telescope and scanning the horizon with their binoculars.

Wanda laughs as she says, "Seems like they've discovered our private beach. I hope they find what they're looking for."

We soon forget all about them and motor out toward the sunken ship.

As we approach the site of the wreck, Wanda looks concerned. Another boat has anchored nearby. She says, "This doesn't look good. That boat is empty. The diver must already be in the water."

"Does that mean trouble?" I ask her.

"Could be," she answers. "There are few secrets kept in the salvage business. Someone thinks there's treasure down there. The law of piracy is, 'First come, First served'. You stay in the boat. I'm going to check on whatever is going on."

She disappears into the water, as brave as any hero I've ever known. Wish I could be more like her.

I wait, and wait, and wait. Whoops, I lean too far over the edge. The boat is rocking...dangerously!

WHOA! I fall back, losing my balance and flop on the floor of the boat.

What is *THAT?*

Straight ahead, I see a monster whale breaking

through the water. He's leaping so high. Now he crashes back under the waves. *Oh no*! The backwash strikes the boat — hard! I grab at nothing. I can't stop myself. I'm falling…

I'M OVERBOARD! I gasp and swallow water. *AIR! I NEED AIR!*

I'm fighting for my life. Am I drowning? Somehow, I reach the surface. I gulp deep breaths. I'm so weak. What to do, what to do? I can barely tread water.

"Wanda, where are you? Help me," I cry. I don't see her anywhere.

YIKES! What I do see chills my bones! Fins, seven of them, surround me. They're circling the boat, cutting the water like sharp butcher knives. I know how many, 'cause I counted the sharks that are coming — for me!

I'M A GONER!

No, not yet. I'm still alive. I scramble to the side of the boat, but can't reach the ladder. I'm too tired. Those fins are getting closer. I can't go on. I GIVE UP!

A shark's nose shoves against me. I close my eyes and wait for its teeth to rip into my flesh.

Wait a minute — my bottom isn't being bitten. It's being pushed back up into the boat. Wanda is saving me. Oh, thank you, Lord!

But it isn't Wanda!

What is it?

It is a dolphin!

A great commotion stirs up the sea. I see dolphins and sharks. The sharks are being rammed and bumped by the dolphins. The sharks are turning toward the open sea…those horrible fins are gone!

One by one, the dolphins show their smiling faces. I can only sit and stare. I watch as those magnificent creatures begin to play. Dancing on the water, they skip on their tails, making bigger and bigger circles around the boat. I hear tweeting and whistling sounds. I don't believe it! I understand what they are saying. I've heard the words before.

The dolphins are singing, *"Seeee, you've learned a lot, Seee, you've laughed a lot, Seee, Wanda's near, Seee, there was nothing to fear."*

"It's true," I call to the dolphins. "I promise I'll never forget."

Several whales break through the water with their calves by their sides. What a sight! The dolphins dip in and out of the water as they escort the whales safely out to sea.

Standing as tall as I can in the rocking boat, I wave, "Aloha, my friends, and Mahalo."

The mystery diver suddenly surfaces. Pulling himself back into his boat, he races off.

But where's Wanda?

Exploding through the water, Wanda swims toward

the ladder, climbs up, then tumbles into the boat. After catching her breath, she exclaims, "That was a close one!"

"What was a close one?" I ask. "What happened down there?"

She tells me, "That guy was just snooping, but he scared himself when he accidentally fired his harpoon gun. Fortunately, it missed us both, lodging in the sand. All I could do was keep waving with my fist until he took off. I'm sure he won't be back. What happened up here?" she asks, loosening her gear.

I start with the whale and keep on going and going — kind of like the Ever Ready Bunny Battery.

Wanda just sits in the boat, staring at me. She looks dumbfounded. "I saw the commotion in the water above me," she says. "But I had to deal with that diver before I could return. Frannie, you are so lucky! What an incredible experience you've had. I'm sorry I missed it." She adds, "I wonder, would the dolphins have done all that if I'd been here?"

"Wanda," I reply. "Let's say our good-byes to DJ and Lucy, and toss the flowers. I think I want to go home now."

Silently, we pay our last respects to DJ and Lucy. The ocean seems to be listening, and becomes calm as we scatter blossoms over the water. It is a very special time. We slowly head back to shore — deep in thought.

Coming ashore, I see that group of whale watchers running toward us. They're jumping up and down like lunatics, and clapping their hands. As I step out of the boat, the first to greet me is the fat lady in the baseball cap.

"What a show! How brave you were. Lucky you, to be out there with those dolphins and whales. They positively loved you," she cries. "We knew you were a special little girl, and we got it all on film. Can't wait to show the folks back home."

After squeezing the life out of me, she asks for my autograph. She hands me a pen and her baseball cap to sign. The others close in, snapping more pictures.

Wanda laughs as she teases me. "May I have your autograph, too, Lucky?"

I can handle fame! Why not give the audience what it wants? So, in my best handwriting, I carefully sign, *'Lucky and Friends.*

LUCKY ME!

Flying home, I remember the gifts of my wonderful trip. I think of Wanda, my very special friend. Her last words to me were, "If you put a *P* in front of *LUCK,* that's how I'll remember you!" Hugging me, she squeezed the 'lucky' locket into my hand, and said, "Lucy and I want you to have this. It was meant to be yours."

I couldn't hold back the tears when I said, "Wanda, I'll wear this locket forever! I'll think of my 'sister' every time I look at it."

I think of that colorful character Jake, alias Captain Hook. We learned a lot from him. I'll always wonder how he lost his leg. I should have asked him when I had the chance. Bet it was an alligator!

I think of those whale and dolphin people. I'm sorry I called them weirdos. They turned out to be great friends. Before we left for the airport, they handed me the pictures they had taken. Big as life in Technicolor, I was in and out of water with dolphins, sharks and whales. Talk about a gift! Wait 'til Helga sees these pictures!

Now Dad knows my story. Wanda told him in part, and I filled him in with every last detail. At first, I thought maybe he didn't believe me 'cause he just sat there shaking his head.

I let Dad look at my locket. "You'll let me keep it, won't you?" I ask.

He says, "I'm so proud of you. Of course you may keep it. You went through a lot! From now on, I'm going to call you, Fearless Frannie! By the way, Frannie," he adds. "I've spoken with the State Department, and they agree that DJ and Lucy have more than earned a medal. They will be receiving it posthumously...since they are no longer alive. We shall invite Wanda to join us in Washington for the ceremony. "

I wanted to cry with joy. I'll see Wanda again soon!

While Dad looks at my pictures, I think about how much I love him. "Aloha Maui, Wanda, whale lovers, Jake, DJ, Lucy, all the magnificent mammals in the Pacific, and *Lucky Lady.* Aloha even to those mean pink anemones, and that quack of a doctor," I whisper.

Over the whine of the engines, Dad calls out, "So,

Fearless, ready for our trip to Egypt?"

"Whoa, back up," I shriek. "The ocean is one thing. No way am I going where pharaohs and mummies haunt pyramids! Don't even think about it, Dad!"

Dad just smiles...

GBP